Oliver Optic

Dolly and I

A Story for Little Folks

Oliver Optic

Dolly and I
A Story for Little Folks

ISBN/EAN: 9783744771450

Printed in Europe, USA, Canada, Australia, Japan

Cover: Foto ©Andreas Hilbeck / pixelio.de

More available books at **www.hansebooks.com**

The Riverdale Books.

DOLLY AND I.

A STORY FOR LITTLE FOLKS.

BY

OLIVER OPTIC,

AUTHOR OF "THE BOAT CLUB," "ALL ABOARD," "NOW OR NEVER," "TRY AGAIN," "POOR AND PROUD," "LITTLE BY LITTLE," &c.

BOSTON:
LEE AND SHEPARD,
(SUCCESSORS TO PHILLIPS, SAMPSON & CO.)
1864.

ELECTROTYPED AT THE
BOSTON STEREOTYPE FOUNDRY.

DOLLY AND I.

I.

Do you know what *envy* means? I hope you have never felt it, for it is a very wicked feeling. It is being sorry when another has any good thing. Perhaps you will know better what the word means when you have read my story; and I hope it will help you to keep the feeling away from your own heart.

Not far from Mr. Lee's house, in Riverdale, lived a man by the name of Green. He was the agent of one of the factories in the village. Mr. Green had two little girls and three sons. The boys have nothing to do with my story, and for that reason I shall not say a great deal about them.

Katy, Mr. Green's older daughter, was ten years old. She was a pretty good girl, but she did not like to have others get good things, when she did not have any herself. If any person gave one of her brothers an apple, or an orange, she seemed to think she ought to have it.

When she was a baby, she

used to cry for every thing she saw, and would give her parents no peace till they gave it to her. I am sorry to say they were sometimes very weak on this point, and gave her things which she ought not to have had, just to quiet her.

Her father and mother hoped, when she grew older, she would not want every thing that belonged to her brothers. If Charles had a plaything, Katy wanted it, and would cry till she got it. Very often, just to make her stop crying, her mother made poor Charley give up the thing.

But as Katy grew older, she seemed to want every thing that others had just as much as ever. She was now ten years old, and still she did not like to see others have any thing which she could not have. It is true she did not

always say so, but she felt it
just as much, and was very
apt to be cross and sullen towards those whom she envied.

Nellie Green was not at all
like her sister. She was only
eight years old, but there was
not a bit of envy in her. She
would give a part, and often
the whole, of her apples,
oranges, candy, and playthings
to her sister, and to her brothers. She liked to see them

happy, and when Charley ate an apple, it tasted just as good to her as though she were eating it herself.

She was not selfish. She would always divide her good things with her friends. Did you ever see a little boy or a little girl eating an apple or some candy, and another little boy or girl standing by, and looking just as if he wanted some?

Nellie always gave her friends a part, and then she not only enjoyed what she ate herself, but she enjoyed what they ate. This is the way to make apples, oranges, and candy taste good.

One New Year's Day, Katy's aunt, after whom she was named, sent her a beautiful wax doll. It was a very pretty doll, and the little girl was the happiest child in Riverdale when the welcome present reached her.

There was another little girl in Riverdale who was almost if not quite as happy; and that was Nellie, her sister. It is true, the doll was not for her; she did not own any of it, and Katy would hardly let her touch it; but for all this, Nellie was pleased to see her sister so happy.

The dolly's name was Lady

Jane; for Katy thought, as she was a very fine doll, she ought to have a very fine name. So, when she spoke to the doll, — and she talked a great deal with her, — she always called her Lady Jane.

The two little girls had five or six other dolls, but none of them were any thing near such fine ladies as Lady Jane. Their heads were made of porcelain, or rubber, or composition, and they had grown so old that they were really ugly.

Miss Lucy, who had a rubber head, looked as though she "had been through the wars." Her nose was worn out, so that she had a great hole in the end of it. I suppose, if she had wanted to sneeze, this hole would have been very handy; but Miss Lucy was a very proper young lady, and never sneezed in company. If she ever sneezed when alone, of course there was no one present to know any thing about it.

There was another hole right in the top of her head, so that if she had had any brains, they would certainly have leaked out; but as Miss Lucy was not a strong-minded woman, I suppose she had no use for brains.

One of the family of dolls was a little black girl, whose name was Dinah. She had seen hard service in her day, and did not look as though she would last much longer.

Miss Fanny had once been a fine lady, but times had gone hard with her, and her fine clothes were both ragged and dirty. But hard times were not so very bad, for she wore the same smile as when her

clothes had been new and
nice.

Miss Mary was a poor crip-
ple. By a sad accident she
had broken one of her legs.
Katy placed her on a table
one day, and either because
the height from the floor
made her dizzy, or because
she was laid too near the
edge, she had tumbled off,
and one leg was so badly
broken that neither a wooden

nor a cork one could be fastened in its place.

Therefore Miss Mary could not walk about the room, and never went any where, except when she was carried. But she was not half so badly off as Miss Susie, who had broken her neck, and lost off her head. The head was tied on with a string, but it kept falling off while the family were at play; but Miss Susie

did not seem to mind it at
all.

She got along a great deal
better without her head than
you and I could without ours.
Indeed, she wore the same
smile upon her face whether
the head was on or off—
which teaches us that we
ought always to be cheerful
in misfortune.

Besides these fine young
ladies there were two or three

rag babies; but as you could not tell by the looks of them what they were thinking about, I will not say any thing about them. They had no virtues worth telling; they never ate soup with a fork, or gave money to the poor.

Some of my readers may not think much of this family of dollies, but I am sure Katy and Nellie had fine times with them. They used to spend hours together with them, and the dollies used to do every thing that any body could do.

Miss Fanny used to visit a great deal, in spite of her dirty, ragged clothes; so did Miss Lucy, with two holes in her head, and Miss Mary, with her broken leg, and Miss Susie, with her broken neck. All of them used to go a-visiting, except Miss Dinah, and she, being a black girl, had to do the sweeping and tend the door.

These ladies were all of them so bashful that they would not speak in company, and Katy and Nellie had to do all the talking for them.

But they used to "make believe" the dollies talked, and this did just as well. They used to say just such things as the ladies did who called on Mrs. Green, and

never left without being urged
to stay longer, and also to
call again; which they always
promised to do.

On the whole, they were
very wonderful dollies; at
least they were until Lady
Jane came, and she was such
a fine lady, with her white silk
dress and her *real* hair, that
none of them could shine after
that.

"Lend us your Dolly."

II.

ONE day Flora Lee came to see Nellie Green, and to spend the afternoon with her. It was in the month of November, and the weather was too cold to permit them to play in the garden; so they said they would have a good time in the house.

Katy Green had to go away,

and could not play with them.
Nellie was very sorry for this,
for she not only liked to have
her sister with her, but she
also wanted the company of
Lady Jane.

She told Flora how sorry
she was, and they agreed that
it was too bad Katy had to
go away, for she was older
than they, and could help
them a great deal in their
plays.   Besides, they wanted

one fine lady among the dollies, for they had a certain play which required just such a person.

"I wish I had brought Miss Dolly with me. I guess she is fine enough," said Flora.

"I wish you had," replied Nellie; "but as you have not, we can't help it now. I dare say Miss Fanny will do."

"I'll tell you what you can do, Nellie."

"What?"

"You can just ask Katy to lend you her dolly. We won't hurt her a mite, you know. We will use her just as if she were made of glass."

Nellie did not know what to say. She did not like to ask Katy to let her play with Lady Jane, for she knew how careful her sister was of her fine lady. And she did not like to tell Flora her thoughts, lest she should think her sister was selfish. She did not like to have any one think hard of her sister.

"We must have Lady Jane. I don't see how we can get along without her," added Flora, a little puzzled by the silence of Nellie.

"I don't like to ask Katy," said Nellie, at last.

"Why not? She will let you have her. Of *course* she

will let you have her," added
-Flora, warmly.

"I don't think she will. You
know we might break her
neck, or lose off her legs or
arms; or we might dirty her
white silk dress."

"But we will be very careful. Let us go and ask her.
It won't do any harm to ask
her, you know. She can't do
any more than refuse."

Nellie did not like to be

refused, and she tried to prevent Flora from going any farther in the matter. She was sorry to have it appear that her sister was selfish, and she thought more of this than she did of being refused.

Flora said so much that at last she thought Katy might let her have the doll, and they ran down stairs to the sitting room, to have the matter settled.

"Will you lend us your dolly, Katy?" asked Nellie, and the tones of her voice showed how doubtful she was of the result of the question.

"What dolly do you mean?" asked Katy.

"Your wax dolly — Lady Jane."

"I am very sure I shall not," replied Katy.

"We will be very careful of her," added Flora. "We won't

let her be hurt a bit — you may depend on that."

"I'm not going to let you have my dolly to break and spoil — I'm sure I shall not," said Katy, who even seemed to be angry because she was asked.

"But don't I say we won't hurt it a bit?" continued Flora. "And when you come over to my house, you shall have my dolly just as long as

you want her; and her house
too, and all the chairs and
tables and things."

"I don't want them."

"Do please to let us have
Lady Jane," teased Nellie.
"We want her ever so much;
and I know she won't get
broken or dirty. Please to
lend her to us, Katy."

"I shan't do any such thing;
so it's no use to tease me.
Why don't you play with your

own dollies? I won't lend Lady Jane — that's flat."

Nellie felt so bad she could not help crying, — not because she could not have the doll, but because her sister was so harsh and unkind. She would not have cared so much if Flora had not been there, for she did not like to have her see her sister behave in this manner.

Poor Flora wanted to cry,

too, when she saw how badly Nellie felt; but she tried to be brave, and placed her arm round her friend's neck, as if to let her know that she would be kind to her.

"Come, Nellie, let's go up stairs again. We won't say any thing more about it," said Flora; and she led her out of the room.

"Now you won't like Katy, after this," replied Nellie.

"O, yes, I will."

"Katy would have lent us the dolly, only aunt Jane gave it to her, and she is afraid it will be broken. If it hadn't been for this, she would have lent us Lady Jane — I know she would," added Nellie, wiping away her tears.

"I dare say she would; but we won't think any thing more about it. And when I come over again, some time, I will bring her something, just to show her that I don't feel hard towards her."

"What a dear, good girl you are, Flora! I was afraid you would hate her after what she said."

"O, dear, no, I should hope not. My mother tells me I must love those who don't do what I want them to; and I try to do so; but it is very hard sometimes. I wish you had a wax doll, Nellie. You ought to have one, you are such a good girl, and love your sister so much, even when she is not kind to you."

"I wish I had one; it would be so nice to have one like Lady Jane. I should be so happy; but then if only one of us can have one, I would rather Katy had it than have it myself."

"You are not a bit selfish,

Nellie.   Do you know what *selfish* means?   I do."

"I guess I do.   It means when you have an apple or any candy to refuse to give a part to your sister."

"Yes, or to any body that happens to be with you.   Candy is good, but don't you like to see others eat it almost as well as you do to eat it yourself?"

"Well, yes, I think I do."

"Then you know just what I mean, and I guess we'll play ' visiting ' now."

"So we will; and Miss Fanny shall be the great lady, and Dinah shall be her servant."

"Yes, and this shall be her house," said Nellie, as she placed Miss Fanny in a large arm chair which they were to "make believe" was her elegant mansion.

"You shall stay here, and I

will bring Miss Mary to visit
Miss Fanny."

Flora bounded over to the
other side of the room, which
was supposed to be the home
of the other dolls, and Miss
Mary, in spite of her broken
leg, was soon on her way to
visit the fine lady.

"Ting, a ling, a ling!" said
Flora, which meant that the
caller had rung the bell, and
Dinah appeared at the door.

"Is Miss Fanny at home?" asked Flora, speaking for the lady with the broken leg.

"No, marm, she is not," replied Nellie, who had to speak for Dinah, because, though her mouth was very large, she could not speak for herself.

"What an awful fib!" cried Flora. "There she is; don't I see her through the door?"

"But that's just the way some of the fine folks do," replied Nellie, laughing at Flora's earnestness.

"It is an awful story, and I wouldn't say it even in fun."

Nellie said she would not say it again, only she wanted to have Miss Fanny do just as the big folks did. And so they played all the afternoon, though Lady Jane did not honor them with her company. All the dollies paid lots of visits; and Flora went home.

The Christmas Present.

III.

WHEN Flora reached home, she told her mother what a nice time she had, and what splendid visits Miss Lucy and Miss Mary and Miss Susie had made to Miss Fanny.

She could not help telling her mother what a good girl Nellie was, and how she loved her sister, even when she was unkind and spoke pettishly to her.

Then she told her how much she wished Nellie had a wax doll, with real hair, and a white silk dress. Mrs. Lee thought such a good girl ought to have one, and the very next time she went to the city, she bought the prettiest wax doll she could find for her.

Flora was full of joy when she saw the doll, and learned

whom it was for. She was a great deal happier than if the doll had been bought for herself; and she wanted to run right over to Mr. Green's with the beautiful present. She longed to see the eyes of Nellie sparkle as she saw the doll, and to hear what she would say when told it was for her. But Mrs. Lee thought they had better keep the doll till Christmas, and let her find it with her stocking in the morning.

"But then I shan't see her when she first gets the dolly," said Flora.

"That is true; but you must write a little note, which shall be pinned on the doll's dress."

"That will be splendid, mother! And I will go right away and write the note now."

Flora got a pencil and a piece of paper, and seated

herself in the corner. She worked away for half an hour as busy as a bee, and then she carried the note to her mother. She was not much of a writer, having been to school only a year. She could only print the note.

Flora was very fond of writing notes, and long before she could make a single letter, she would fill up a piece of paper with pothooks and spiders' legs, and send them to her mother and Frank.

She did not spell all the words right, but her mother told her how to correct them, and then she printed the note over again, on a nice sheet of gilt-edged paper. Thinking my little friends might want to see this note, I place a copy of it in the book, just exactly as she wrote it.

Dear Nellie

This
Dolly IsFrom Me.
I Love You Very
Much And I Wish
You A Merry
Christmas.

Flora Lee.

When Christmas morning came, Nellie found the doll in a chair, close by her stocking. I can't tell you how pleased she was, but you can all guess. Then she took the note from the dress, and read it. She was more pleased than ever to find it was from Flora.

She almost cried with joy as she puzzled out the note, and thought how kind Flora

and her mother were to re-
member her.

"What a dear you are, Miss
Dolly!" said she, as she took
up the doll and kissed her,
just as though she had been
a real live baby. "You and
I shall be first-rate friends,
just as long as we live. I will
take such good care of you!
Dear me! Why, mother! Only
think!"

"What is the matter, Nellie ? " asked Mrs. Green, who was almost as much pleased as her daughter.

" Did you see that ? "

" What, child ? What do you mean ? "

" Did you see those eyes? "

" Yes, I see them."

" Why, just as true as I am alive, she moved them ! "

" I think not, my child. She is a very handsome doll, but I don't think she could move her eyes, if she tried ever so hard."

"But she did; I know she did;" and Nellie took hold of her head to examine it more closely. As she did so, she bent the body a little. "There! as true as I live, she moved them again!"

Mrs. Green took the doll, and found that the eyes did really move. It was funny, but it was true. Mrs. Lee

and Flora knew all about it.
The eyes were made of glass,
and there was something in-
side of the doll which moved
them when the body was bent.

"Let me see," said Katy,
who had been looking on in
silence all this time. Nellie
gave her the doll at once;
and she bent the body and
saw the eyes move twenty
times. The happy owner of
Miss Dolly waited with pa-

tience till her sister had done
with her.

"Why didn't aunt Jane get
me one like that, I wonder,"
said Katy, when she gave the
doll to Nellie.

"I suppose she could not
afford to buy one like this, for
she is not so rich as Mrs. Lee."

"But you shall have her to
play with just when you want
her," said Nellie.

"Pooh! I don't want your

old dolly," snarled Katy. "She isn't half so good as mine. I would rather have Lady Jane than have her, any day."

"Why, then, did you wish your aunt Jane had given you one like this?" asked her mother.

"I don't care for her old dolly! She may keep it for all me," replied Katy.

"But it shall be yours just as much as mine, Katy," said

Nellie, in tones so gentle and sweet that her sister ought to have kissed her for them, and loved her more than she ever loved her before.

But she did not. She was envious. She was sorry the doll had been given to Nellie — sorry because it was a prettier one than her own. It was a very wicked feeling. She had some presents of her own, but her envy spoiled all the pleasure she might have taken in them.

Nellie was almost sorry the doll had been given to her, when she saw how Katy felt about it.   Mrs. Green talked to the envious girl till she cried, about her conduct.   She tried to make her feel how odious and wicked envy made her.

Whenever Katy saw the new doll, she seemed to be

angry with her sister. Poor Nellie's pleasure was nearly spoiled, and she even offered to exchange her doll for Katy's, but her mother would not let her do so.

In a few days, however, she seemed to feel better, and the two sisters had some good times with their dolls. I say she seemed to feel better, but she really did not. She did not like it that Nellie's doll was a finer one than her own.

Yet Nellie was happier, for she thought Katy was cured of her ill feeling. Then she loved her doll more than ever. She was a cunning little girl, and she thought so much of her new friend that she always used to say "Dolly and I."

When her mother asked her where she had been, she would reply, "Dolly and I have been having a nice time up stairs." "Dolly and I" used to do ever so many things, and no two little ladies could ever enjoy themselves more than did Dolly and Nellie.

I am sorry to say that Katy did not like Dolly at all. She could never forgive her for moving her eyes, because Lady Jane could not move hers. It is true that, after she saw how silly and wicked her envy made her appear to others, she tried very hard not to show it.

We may be just as wicked without showing our sin to others, as we can be when we let the world see just what we are. When we are wicked, the sin is more in the heart than in the actions.

Men may seem to be very good when they are really very bad, though people almost always find out such persons. Katy was just as wicked, just as envious, when her sister thought she was kind and loving, as she was on that Christmas morning, when the doll was found in the chamber.

You will be, surprised and sorry when you see just how wicked her envy made her. I shall tell you about it in the next chapter, and I hope it will lead you to drive any such feeling from your own hearts. If you have such feelings, they will make you very unhappy; and the sooner you begin to get rid of them, the better.

What Katy did.

IV.

LADY JANE and Miss Dolly were kept in the lower drawer of the bureau, for they were very fine young ladies, and Mrs. Green wished to have them kept clean and nice.

One day, about two weeks after Miss Dolly was given to Nellie, both she and Katy had been playing with the dolls.

When the bell rang for tea, they ran down stairs; but before they went they put the dolls in the drawer. As they were in a hurry, they were not very careful, and the dresses of both the dolls were sadly tumbled.

Mrs. Green, who was in the room, saw in what manner Miss Dolly and Lady Jane had been thrown into the drawer; and before she went down to tea, she took them both out, smoothed down their dresses, and put them back in a more proper manner.

Katy and Nellie had had some talk about their dolls; and the envious girl had said hers was better than her sister's. Nellie did not dispute with her about it, but she saw that Katy had not got over that bad feeling yet.

The children ate their sup-

pers, and not a word more
was said about the dolls; but
Katy looked very sour. She
was thinking about Miss Dolly's eyes, and wishing Lady
Jane's eyes would move like
the other's.

She finished her supper, and
ran up stairs again. By this
time it was quite dark in the
room where the dolls were
kept, and Nellie and her
mother wondered why she

went up stairs at that late hour.

Katy was still thinking of those eyes. She thought her aunt Jane was real mean not to buy her such a doll; and then she was very sorry that Flora's mother had bought it for her sister.

While she was thinking these wicked thoughts she went to the bureau, and opened the lower drawer. It was so dark

she could hardly see the dolls,
but she took out one of them.

"Your dolly shall not be
better than mine any longer,"
said she to herself.

As she said this, she took
the scissors from the work
basket on the bureau, and
finding one of the eyes with
her fingers, she struck one of
the points right into it. Then
she turned the scissors, so as
entirely to destroy the eye.

Not content with this, she spoiled the other eye in the same manner.

"Now your doll isn't so good as mine, any how," said she to herself, as she put the poor spoiled lady back into the drawer.

I would not have a little girl feel as she felt then for all the world. Her heart was full of envy and wickedness. To gratify her ill feeling she had thrust the scissors into the eyes of the doll. She knew how badly her sister would feel, but she did not care for this. Now Lady Jane was the best doll, and she did not care for any thing else.

She staid in the room but a few moments. Closing the drawer, she hastened down stairs, and took a seat by the fire. She tried to look as though nothing had happened; but she was sour and sullen, for she felt that she had done a very naughty act.

"Come, Katy; let us go up stairs, and play with the dollies again," said Nellie, when she had got through with her supper.

"I don't want to," replied she, without even looking at her sister.

"Do come, Katy."

"I tell you I don't want to," snarled she.

"You can bring your dolly down stairs, and play with her here, Nellie," said her mother.

"May I, mother?"

"You may — take a light with you."

"I don't want any light, mother; I can find her just as well in the dark;" and away she ran to get the doll.

Don't you think Katy trembled then? She did tremble, like a leaf, and wished she had not done the naughty deed. In a moment Nellie would return with poor Miss Dolly, whose eyes had been spoiled with the scissors. She did not think it would be found out so soon, and she could not think what to say before the doll came down.

She felt just as though she should sink through the floor,

when Nellie came into the room with the doll in her arms. There would be an awful time in a moment, and her father and mother would want to know who had spoiled Miss Dolly's eyes.

They knew she had been up stairs since tea, and they would charge her with the naughty act. She meant to deny it, for those who are wicked enough to do such things are almost always wicked enough to lie about them.

"Now won't you and I have a nice time, Dolly?" said Nellie, as she rushed into the sitting room, with the doll in her arms. "Come, Katy, let's play Dolly is the queen of England."

"I don't want to play."

"Well — won't you make me a crown for her?"

"I can't."

Katy was waiting for her sister to find out the mischief that had been done, and she dreaded the moment when she should do so. She did not dare to look at her, for fear her looks might betray her.

"You shall be queen without any crown," said Nellie, as she placed the doll on the table. "This pincushion shall be your throne. There, you look just like a queen — don't she, mother?"

"I think she does," replied Mrs. Green, with a smile. "I hope she will be as good as Queen Victoria."

"She will, mother — only she ought to have a crown."

"I have got a piece of gilt paper up stairs, and I will make her one. I'm going up in a minute."

Katy, not daring to look

yet, did not know what to
think of this talk.   How could
the doll look like a queen when
her eyes had been punched
out with the scissors?   It was
very strange to her, and she
stole a glance at the queenly
Miss Dolly on the table.

There she was, seated on
her pincushion throne, just as
if nothing had happened.   Her
eyes were just as bright as
ever, and as Nelly bent her

body, she moved them as well as ever she could.

Katy did not know what to make of it. She had certainly driven the scissors into the eyes of the doll as hard as she could; but there was Miss Dolly as good as new. She could not explain it, and it was of no use to try.

Mrs. Green brought down the scissors, and cut out the crown. Then Miss Dolly certainly looked like a queen, and Nelly spent a very pleasant hour with her majesty, till it was time for her to go to bed.

Katy was very unhappy. She had not done what she meant to do, and she was filled with doubt. But she did not have to wait long to find out what she had done. When Mrs. Green went up stairs with the children, Miss

Dolly had to be put to bed first, for she was a queen.

When the bureau drawer was opened, what do you think they saw? There lay Lady Jane, with both of her eyes punched out!

Katy burst into tears when she saw that her doll was entirely spoiled. Then she found that she had made a mistake. In the darkness she had punched out the eyes of Lady

Jane instead of Miss Dolly. This is the way that wicked people often punish themselves instead of others.

Her mother had changed the places of the dolls in the drawer, and this was the reason why Katy had made the mistake. Don't you think it served her right?

Katy felt so badly that she could not tell any of the lies she had made up, and the truth was found out by her mother. Mrs. Green scolded her for what she had done, and for what she meant to do. The naughty girl cried herself to sleep that night, but poor Lady Jane was utterly ruined.

Nellie felt almost as bad as her sister, and said all she could to console her. The next day Katy was so ashamed of herself that she did not wish to see any body. But in a few

days she got over it; and her
mother hoped the affair would
do her a great deal of good.
Whenever she showed a spirit
of envy, Mrs. Green reminded
her of her doll, and she tried
to conquer the feeling; but it
took many years to cure her.

When you envy others, al-
though you may not punch out
the eyes of your own doll, you
hurt yourself more than any
one else.